FIRE BY KNIGHT

By Aaron Dowen

First paperback edition October 2020

Book design by Aaron J. Dowen

ISBN: 9798689573526

Published by Catalyst Comics Studio
www.catalystcomicsstudio.com

7 March, 1103

I remember the sky, the blood orange moon as it fell over the mountains. My breath caught in my chest as I ran with everything I had. The muscles in my legs burned like fire, but my feet were not stopping. I knew that this night would change my story and would decide my future. What I had seen nearly froze me in place, but I was raised with a sense of responsibility. A responsibility my father taught me to have for myself, my family, and our people. So, rather than coiling in fear and dying in cowardice, I ran. I remember the feeling of my heart bursting against my rib cage, and my brain dizzying in distress. I had to make it. I had to warn everyone. The war was coming right for us, and I wasn't convinced we would be able to stop it.

Airic stumbled through the brush, pushing past the edge of the woods into the clearing at the edge of town. His initial reaction was to scream, but he suppressed it, knowing that it would only cause chaos. The light was nearly gone now, and Airic's eyes were already in a blur from the sweat pouring from his forehead. He did not see the short, wooden fence before slamming into it, causing him to tumble over its side. Lifting himself up, he felt a searing pain pierce through his body. The agony was intense, but he refused to let it distract him from getting to his father. As he turned the corner onto the street, he could see his home at the end of it, beckoning him to push forward.

Bursting through the front door, Airic began to scream for his father. Instead, he was greeted by his mother as she rushed to the doorway, shushing him.

"You will wake your sister! Where have you been?" She hissed at him and glared with tired eyes.

"Where is Father? I need to speak to him...Mom, get Sarai ready to leave." Her face began to turn as she noticed the seriousness in his tone. She scanned him up and down, seeing the rip in his pants, letting the blood drop to the ground.

"Airic, what is happening? What happened to your leg?" Their conversation was interrupted as Arden, Airic's father rushed down the steps. Arden was awakened from his sleep; but to his son, he still
looked every bit the nobleman the rest of the world saw him as.

"Son, what is it?"

"On the other side of the woods... men with torches and swords... coming this way." Airic watched as his father's eyes darted around the room. He turned away to his wife and put his hands on her shoulders.

"Evelyn, take the kids and get as far away from here as you

can. Pack only what you can carry, and nothing heavy." He placed his forehead against hers; they maintained eye contact for a moment before he finally pushed her away. She moved quickly up the stairs, as Arden ran through the room to the armory.

"Father, I want to stay to help fight. I want to protect Vanhal!" Arden disregarded his presence and began to place his armor over his shoulders.

"Airic, I need you to run as hard as you can to the tower... Williford must ring the bell. We have to get the people to safety."

"But, father..."

"Go, now son!" Airic turned and grimaced as he became aware of the pain in his leg once again. He began to jog, pushing through the doorway and out onto the street. He looked back to the woods, where he had emerged from, and in the distance, he could see a faint glow of torches. There was not much time left, causing Airic to break into a sprint. By this time, his leg was throbbing in pain.

The stone church cast a long shadow in the new moonlight, covering the road leading to it in darkness. Airic pushed open the great wooden doors and screamed for Williford, the groundskeeper.

"Father Williford! Ring the bell! We are under attack!"

Silence...

"Father Williford, we have to ring the bell, now!"

Silence...

Airic rushed to the stairway and began his ascent to the bell tower. If it had not been for the torches, he would have slipped immediately on the dark stone steps. He rushed to the top of the tower and stopped for a moment as he could now see the entire village laid out before him. As his eyes met the tree line, he could see the flames of the torches, no longer just a glow. He spun around and looked up to the dark bell hanging over him. Reaching up, he fumbled to find the rope in the darkness, frantically swinging it once it did. The bell was loud, causing his ears to ring. He found enough concentration to scream.

"Everyone, run! Get as far from here as you can! They are coming from the woods!" His voice cracked in the cool night air. Whether it was the bell's piercing ring or the shriek of terror in his voice, the roads began to fill with people running. The torches edged closer to the city. Airic looked in horror as he saw the first house erupt into flames, casting a glow down the street. He was frozen in place, afraid to let go of the rope. He could now see the attackers as they made their way onto the main streets. He watched as the men stood against them to buy their families time. The sound of the bell was replaced by the screams of men, women, and children, the clanking of metal, and the crackling of fire.

A swooshing sound slipped through the air where Airic stood. He reached up and touched his face, it was cold and wet. Blood, he thought before finally releasing the rope and launching himself to cover behind the stone slabs near the staircase. He rushed down the steps, eager to find his father and fight alongside him. He slipped through the chapel to the doorway, running directly into a large man as he did. As he looked up, he could see the rage in the man's eyes, and the soot covering his face. The man raised his arm, then thrust it down, crushing the hilt of his sword against Airic's head. The world began to spin, blood slipped over his eyes, and he blacked out.

Airic awakened to the sound of metal being crushed together, blended with the grunts of men as they battled. He struggled to move his arms but knew instantly that his hands were tied together. He squinted his eyes as they began to adjust to the light. He felt the warmth of the sun on his face. As his eyes focused, he realized it was deep into the night, and the light was that of the buildings of his village burning. He had been moved, no doubt by the ogreish man that knocked him unconscious. He was near the edge of the village, and he could see the church in the distance as he began to sit up. Flames leaped from the bell tower, stones crumbled and fell as he watched. It was his father's voice that snapped him back into the present.

"Go, leave this place. We have nothing worth taking!" His father's voice sounded rough like he had been drinking fire. Airic fell to the ground and rolled to get a better look. His father was kneeling on the ground with his hands tied behind his back. His armor covered in blood and dirt, a deep gash in his forehead allowed blood to cascade down his face. Still, he was resilient, his teeth clenched in anger, his chest out and body tensed. The man standing near him was busy talking to his subordinates, issuing commands. Airic had to get his father's attention. He had to help find a way out of this.

"Father..." he spoke lightly, his words caught in the air as his throat was too dry. His father heard enough to turn in his direction.

"Airic, son, find your mother and sister. Tell every knight you pass what has happened here." The man turned to face his father. He nodded with a grimace on his face, rubbing his gloved hands together.

"Sir Arden... you are correct. There is nothing worth our time in this village. Luckily, the price was... pre-negotiated." Airic watched as his father braced a foot to the ground and launched himself into the man.

"RUN AIRIC!" Arden screamed as he kicked the man ferociously, gathering the attention of the other guards. Airic got to his feet and ran as hard as he could into the woods. He knew the next township where his mother and the village would be running to. As he turned back to see if he was being chased, he saw the beast of a man stand to his feet and forcefully hit Arden over the head. Arden fell to his knees as the man took a sword from his guardsmen and lifted it over his head with two hands pointing the blade down toward his chest. Airic's face turned to horror as the man plunged the blade into his father's chest, slashing through the armor and out through the back.

Airic's blood began to boil. He could feel the sensation of fire pulse through his veins. He ran toward the men, unsure how far he would get, but he was unable to control his rage. The warrior turned as he heard Airic's scream, first ready to strike him down, but his face quickly changed to confusion.

"What is this witchcraft?!" The barbarian shouted, fumbling for a sword, but never breaking eye contact.

Airic charged forward, he felt the rope holding his hands together snap. His head swam with a wave of newfound anger, a power he had never felt this strongly before. He closed the distance to the man; and, leaping over his father's lifeless body, he tackled the giant. A loud Tsssss sound coursed through the air, and he fell to the ground in a roll. As he stood to face the man again, he turned to find nothing but a pile of ash, with a glowing metal sword laying on the ground. The other warriors had turned now, braced for an attack and a command from their leader. What they saw brought terror like a wave into the air.

"What is this?" One screamed. They each took a step back, leaning their weight on their heels.

Airic looked in confusion all around him; then, catching a glimpse of his hands, he looked down. His skin was glowing, the veins in his wrist were radiating bright yellow. He looked at the men in confusion, before looking at the pile of ash on the ground. Anguish washed over him as he realized he had killed the man. He had no time to think though, the battle wasn't over.

"Archers! Take him out!" A voice rang through the silence.

Airic looked up at the men, feeling the rage building inside again. They stepped aside, making way for the archers to step forward. He watched as they pulled their bowstrings tight, aiming arrows at him. He thought he would do more, take more of them out. If nothing else, he had bought time for his people to get farther away. He lifted his hands in front of his face and looked away.

"FIRE!" A man shouted.

"Noooo!" Airic screamed as he heard the arrow's release and whizz through the air. He squeezed his eyes tightly shut as he awaited the pain to overtake him. There was nothing though, and his first thought was that he must be dead. He opened his right eye first, seeing only the ground. He looked up, at last, dropping his hand to his side, as the image before him tore the breath from his chest. *Ashes... everything is ashes.* Where men stood, singed grass and sparking dirt remained.

21 June, 1104

It has been over a year now. My father is dead, and I was never able to find my mother. I still believe she is alive, the people in the next village had seen her. I have been searching, but spending most of my time doing odd jobs to survive. Still, a woman gave me a small leather case with paper inside. She told me to write in it, that it would help in dealing with what comes in the future. In my downtime, I hideaway in the forest, practicing with this magic that flows through me. I struggle to control it but have learned to bring enough water to put out any accidental fires I have started. I have kept this power hidden, but I want to learn more... and there might be a way now that I can.

The storm forced Airic to find shelter in the horse stables. It was muggy, smelled of hay and feces, and was a bit damp, but he would rather be inside than out in the rain. He placed his journal back into his bag, then closed the ink and wrapped it with the quill in a loose piece of fabric. As he lay down, his head began to spin, as it had every night since the day his village fell. He waited for the storm to subside and stared through the wooden slates above him. He could see the light of the moon as the sky began to clear. He wondered if his mother and sister could be looking at the same time as him. He forced his eyes shut and clutched his hand around the bag beside him. He knew if he pushed through the thoughts and memories that eventually, he would drift off to sleep.

Shouts from the street shook Airic from his sleep, causing him to leap up, his arm glowing bright yellow. He listened intently, searching through the echoes to decipher the words. It was the voice of an older man, gruff and rattling, shouting that he is looking for someone. Unthreatened, Airic shook his hand, allowing the glow to subside and his brain to regain its composure. He strapped his bag over his arm and opened the stable doors. He stepped out into the rain and let it wash over his face as he began his walk toward the voice.

"Is there anyone here from Vanhal?" the man shouted. Airic began to pick up his pace, eager to find out what the man knew.

"Anyone at all? I have some things from the village..."

Airic was on the next street over, unable to contain his excitement, he screamed.

"I am, I am from Vanhal! My name is Airic, and my father was Lord Arden!"

As he turned the corner, his eyes met with the man on the horse. Even better, he knew this man; it was the familiar face of

Father Williford. Yet, something was different now, where his face had once been full of joy and peace, now looked solemn and aged. After a moment, his eyes began to lighten and expand. He kicked his foot over the side of the horse and dropped down to the ground, running toward Airic. As their distance closed, they embraced each other, and Father Williford began to sob.

"Airic, you are alive... you are alive!" He exclaimed between his tears. Silence hung in the air for a moment, broken only by the huffing of the preacher's horse.

"Father Williford... where were you? I ran to the bell tower to find you, but you weren't there?" There was a twinge of resentment in Airic's tone.

"I was in the woods when I saw the army, but they were between me and the village. By the time I made it back, everyone had fled...or was taken. I spent a year in shame, living in a ruined village. Finally, I packed up the things I could find and headed here."

"I injured my leg, and they tried to take me, but, I... I got away."

"Did anyone else make it here? I thought everyone would have come here..." His eyes darted around, searching for another familiar face.

"I... I think they moved on. It took me nearly a month to make it here. I was lost and had no horse. I have been here ever since, waiting to see if anyone came back for me."

The preacher hugged Airic's shoulders again, and pulling back, revealed a light smile on his face.

"Airic, I have something that belonged to your father." The preacher turned and began to rummage through the cart, pushing over singed heirlooms from the village. Finally, he lifted out a familiar shape, about two feet wide and two feet tall. He turned to Airic and handed it to him from the cart. Airic's eyes brightened, and tears began to form as he grasped onto the wooden planks, painted with his family coat of arms. He hadn't even noticed Father Williford standing beside him on the ground.

"This is more than just a memory son, this is your family coat of arms, which has your father's name inscribed on the back. Under his name, is yours..."

"I use to look at this all the time; it hung above my father's armor... His fingers used to trace over the etched shapes of the dragon and lion figures. Both figures faced a shield with a flame in the middle."

"This is a symbol of your nobility. You need to be taken to King Henry to be trained by the kingdom. It would be a much better life than you have here."

"What about my family? I still have to find my sister and mother."

"The best way to find them is to become a knight, with access to an army with knowledge of where people are. Don't you see son? This is a chance for you to make things right."

"I will go, for my father, and to honor my family."

As Airic turns to climb into the cart, Father Williford stops him. Leaning in to whisper to him.

"There is something we have to talk about... Something I overheard the army talking about before the attack. I think they were sent there by someone on our side. I've been trying to piece together everything I heard ever since, and I think someone had found out about your father..."

"My father? He was a warrior, always looking out for our village. What purpose would they have in destroying everything?"

"Your father was a very different kind of warrior... a special project commissioned by the King, himself. Not everyone knew about his abilities, and some of those that did know did not approve."

"What kind of abilities?"

Father Williford ushered Airic into the back of the cart, his eyes darting around to anyone that walked past them.

"We will talk when we get out of the city. Your father was a special man, and it made him extremely valuable. More than you could know…"

The cart lunged forward, leaving Airic alone with his thoughts as they pushed toward the outskirts of the village. Could my father have had the same powers as me? Who knew about it? Will they come for me too?

17 January, 1113

It has been nearly ten years now since the fall of my village. I had met the King, along with Father Williford, who established and confirmed my nobility. I began my training and was thrust into battle within my first four months. I was fifteen when I cut a man down for the first time, and by the time I was sixteen, it would not even cause a second thought. As the years passed, I gave up the search for my mother and sister, replacing it instead with the search for answers on who had killed my father. For now, the secret of my powers is safe, only Father Williford knows. What I know now is that the attack ten years ago was not random...

Airic stood his ground, his feet pressed hard into the dirt as men, covered in the blood of battle, raged toward him. The sounds of war were deafening, intensified by the echoing of the valley. Boulders and flaming arrows flew overhead, followed only by the screams of their victims. The first man ran straight for him, leaving himself vulnerable as he raised his sword above his head. Airic ducked, causing the man's legs to slam into his armor, launching him in the air. As he did, Airic turned on his heels, thrusting his blade up from his side. The man fell with a grunt and a thud, unmoving, his sword stuck into the ground in front of him.

The second man pushed his shield into Airic as his sword came down, blocked by the metal gauntlets on his arm. Airic pressed his leg into the bottom of the shield, reaching beneath it, he pulled it up, forcing the ridge into the man's face. The man struggled before falling backward, allowing Airic to force the shield against the man's throat with enough time to meet the blade of another soldier...

The sound of the two swords striking rose over the battlefield, the thunderous exchange pushing the two men in opposite directions. Airic fell on his back, sinking into the blood-soaked mud. His arm was shaking, and his muscles seemed to burn. He could see the faint glow of fire beneath his armor. The other soldier was on his side, in shock from the force as he grasped his own arm. Airic made eye contact with the man as the two began to struggle on the wet ground to get to their feet. His eyes fell to the ground where he saw a streak of ice leading to where they had just been standing. The man followed his eyes, then looked up at Airic in horror, his secret revealed. Both men's eyes moved to Airic's arm, as it began glowing brighter beneath his armor. The man lunged forward, stretching out his arm as a blade of ice to formed over his armor. Airic shielded the blow with his now glowing gauntlet, a hiss of steam and vapor erupted into the air.

The men battled with a sword in one hand and releasing their powers with the other. Airic released an arc of fire from his hand, letting it crash down on them both. As the steam covered their vision, he swiped with his sword and missed. As their eyesight began to clear, they each stood, braced for battle. Their eyes locked, and Airic allowed his blade to trace over the dirt.

"Who are you?" He said as his arm began to glow again.

"My name is Morcant, your powers, how long?" His accent was thicker, leaving Airic to imagine where he might be from.

"Ten years, and you?"

"Fourteen, I was in an accident..." The man formed an ice shield, covering everything but his head. Airic tightened the grip around his sword, preparing to launch back into Morcant.

"I've never met anyone else with powers..."

"I have..." Morcant replied coldly, his eyes fixed on his enemy's blade. Airic's brain raced as he needed to know more and wasn't sure if this man would end the fight. He tried to calm himself, to let the fire subside, but the sounds of the surrounding battle kept him on edge. He focused on Morcant and slowly laid his blade down; his knee pressed into the ground.

"I want no more of this fight... I want to learn more about the others with these powers."

Morcant's eyes shifted as he contemplated the situation. The moment became frozen in time as the two men raced to gather their thoughts. Neither knew what would happen if they continued to fight, but both knew it would only end in more bloodshed. The prospect of discovering more about their powers, and others with similar abilities, drove Morcant to lay his sword down and kneel. For a moment, the two simply stared, unsure if their battle was over.

Airic stood, offering Morcant a hand as he closed the distance between them. He was hesitant at first, but finally grasped

Airic's hand and stood beside him.

"You follow me," Morcant said, not waiting for a response as he began to dash toward the tree line.

The sound of the battle was falling into the distance, and neither man knew who was victorious. They each walked in silence for a long time, finding it difficult to begin a discussion about something each had hidden for so many years. It was Morcant who broke the quiet.

"Your family know your powers?" He never looked back at Airic, only kept walking.

"No... I... I could not bear them with that knowledge."

"That sounds... difficult."

"Sharing this blessing with no one? Having to hide it and only use it when wicked men say. Yes...difficult."

Airic stumbled to keep up with Morcant, the woods becoming denser as the duo slipped further away from the battle. A day had already passed, and the men still had not said much to one another. They killed a pair of rabbits for dinner the night before, allowing the fire to slowly burn while the moon was bright enough to cover the brightness of the flame. They each took turns sleeping, though neither of them rested. The trust only lasted as far as they have known each other, which was still fresh. In the morning, they awoke and made their way through the hills.

"Where are you taking me?" Airic asked, his guard still up.

"To my home" Morcant responded.

"How long have you been away?" Airic wondered, as his feet slipped along the grass.

"Two years now." Morcant kept his answers brief, Airic knew the small talk meant nothing.

"You are seasoned for battle, much more than two years."

"I have been in battle many times in my life, and it never gets easier."

"Why do you fight for the barbarians?" Airic asks, unsure how the man would take his question.

"I have fought for many different leaders, but never by my own choice." Morcant shot back. Airic quietly walked through the thoughts over in his mind. He could not understand how someone could fight for something they did not believe in.

He was so deep in thought that he had not even realized they moved out of the woods and into a clearing. A plain-looking wooden home is all that stood near the top of the hill. As he looked around, he saw a barn in the distance, and not far, was a small stream at the bottom of a hill.

Morcant had made it a ways ahead of him and was almost to the door of the house. Airic watched as he knocked. The door creaked open, and he could almost make out the face of the young girl looking up at Morcant. He could not quite hear their brief exchange of words, but in a moment, she was fully embraced in his arms. Airic slowed down, watching as another figure appeared and embraced him tightly. After a moment, they all turned to Airic as he neared the doorway.

"This is Airic, a nobleman from the king's army," Morcant spoke, gesturing to him.

"Is he a prisoner, daddy?" The young girl asked, causing a smirk to creep up on the adult's faces.

"No, he is just a bit... lost." Morcant gestured for Airic to step closer. "This is my wife, Alara, and my daughter, Elyana."

Airic reached out his hand to Alara, but Elyana grabbed it and shook it instead. Alara nodded to him and turned to walk back into the house. Elyana chased her mother in and began asking questions about the strange man that her father had captured.

Morcant turned and began his walk down the hill to the barn. As they entered, Morcant turned to address Airic.

"This will be your quarters," he said.

"I've slept in worse," Airic responded as he looked around.

"I will get you some blankets, as the nights here can be pretty cold."

Airic held his hand up and let it glow. "I can usually manage it." He smiled as Morcant simply nodded in response.

The evening moved along quickly as Airic gathered with Morcant's family to eat supper. He was careful not to mention anything about their powers, or of the battle between the two. After bathing in the stream, Airic made his way to the barn. There, Morcant had left him a spare tunic and some other clothes, blankets, and a bucket.

As he settled in for the evening, he laid out his sword beside him, along with the few items he carried in his tunic. The knock on the wooden barn door startled him, snapping him back into reality from his thoughts.

Morcant slid the door open and held two large metal cups up, nodding toward Airic. Airic shifted over toward a set of barrels and sat as Morcant met him, handing him the glass. Airic looked at it, smelling the pungent odor of alcohol as he swirled the glass.

"What is this?" Airic asked.

"Something to keep you warm." Morcant smiled as he sat across from him. He took a long draw from the cup, and Airic followed suit. He could feel the warmth grow in his throat and felt it as the alcohol burned its way down to his stomach. His initial reaction caused him to nearly spit it out, but he pushed passed it and finished off the pint.

"So, can you tell me a bit more about... the things you can do?" Airic gestures at Morcant as he places his mug on the ground.

Morcant looks at him for a moment, almost as if studying him.

"I was eleven, the first time. It was a long time ago. I remember being in control one moment, out playing in the woods, and then ice was everywhere. I kept it to myself, but eventually, my parents found out. Then, my father showed me that he too could do it---"

"Are you saying it was something passed down in your bloodline?" Airic's voice exposed the shocked tone he was trying to conceal.

"I see you did not know. Well, it seems to be, from what I have seen." Morcant's voice sounded firm, assured in his knowledge.

"There are others?"

"I have known there to be a few, for better or worse."

"With powers... like ours?"

"Some, I had met a few men with mine, others able to turn their arms to stone. Only one other have I met who could make fire", his eyes narrowed as he looked at Airic.

"You knew my father?" Airic's voice cracked, betraying him.

"I knew a man who could do the same as you. Who also worked for your king."

"How? How did you know him?" The barn was quiet and, the only sounds were of wind rustling the leaves outside. Morcant looked down and sighed.

"There was a battle, not unlike the one I met you in. I used my powers when your father stopped me. I was taken prisoner and brought before the king. Then I was offered a choice; to use my powers for the king or to live as a prisoner. I fought alongside your father and a small group of others who had abilities. I had discovered years later about his passing."

"How did you escape?" Airic asked, his interest peaked.

"I did not. I was told to leave after a bloodbath that cost

your king a lot of men. It was unlike anything I had ever seen. We seemed unstoppable until we were overwhelmed. I came home, and then I was forced into servitude again for another tyrant." The disdain on the breath of Morcant was blatant.

Airic spread his palm across the fabric of his tunic, a conscious attempt to keep him from clenching it.

"The king is a good man", Airic said calmly.

"The king is just a man. You dismiss him because he leads you, but under his hand, your father died."

"It was not by his hand. We were in a village already ruled by him."

"Peculiar then, that such a force could envelop the city without being noticed. Surely anywhere else, there would have been an army amassed."

"It was a surprise attack, cowardly and without regard to any women or children." Airic's voice was turned up in anger now.

"Cowardly, I agree. I am just telling you that your father's unique ability also made him a target."

Airic fell quiet for a moment, thinking of the possibility. The king had been a friend to his father. It would have made no sense for him to have him executed, at the cost of a whole village at that. Morcant has to be mistaken, driven by his own mistrust. He decided to let it go, as Morcant rose to his feet.

"I believe this is enough conversation for the evening. We shall speak in the morning." Morcant nodded, assuring himself as he left the barn.

Airic shuffled out of the barn in the early hours of the morning. He made his way down to the small stream, a leather flask in his hand. As he knelt by the water, his eyes moved over the scenery around him. He could see hills in the distance and the mountains behind those. Around him, there was the clearing, hundreds of acres wide, and leading into another section of the forest. It was quiet and quaint. Airic imagined himself living on the land, hidden away from war, able to use his powers whenever he saw fit.

He looked down as his hand grew colder, now encased in ice. The ground under his feet had turned to frost, and he slipped, falling backward. He could hear chuckling behind him, a gruff voice finding delight at his expense. Airic leaped up to his feet and faced Morcant, who was holding his stomach and laughing.

"I-I am sorry." He said through his cackling.

"How do you have so much control?" Airic asked, spending no thought on the embarrassment, but instead looking at his own hands. "I have tried for years, and I can still only maintain control depending on my anger."

Morcant looked at him, nodded, and placed his hand on his own chin as if sizing up the man standing before him.

"It takes much practice not just over your powers, but over your mind." He finally said as he placed his forefinger to his temple. "Show me..." He offered.

Airic shifted his weight and placed his arm out. His skin turned a bright orange, then white, before finally bursting into flames and launching up to the sky. He held it there, allowing his other arm to be engulfed in flames as well. The edges of his shirt sleeves were singed, burned away from the heat. Morcant paced around him, examining him as if he were an experiment.

"Okay, now lower intensity" Morcant demanded.

Airic looked at his hands with a vivid intensity. He was focused, concentrating on his own powers. The flames along his arms flickered, waning ever slightly before returning to the former. Morcant approached him, making him shift uneasily on one foot.

Morcants arm was also outstretched, a cold fog flowing toward Airic's hands. The heat and cold erupted into steam as they touched, but Airics flame began to diminish. It hovered a foot from his hand at its highest point.

"Ah, see? Feel that? Find that bit of control, and you can have the fire work for you, not have you chained to it." He smiled, assured of himself.

Morcant moved his hands away, but the flames stayed low.

"You are doing that yourself now."

Airic could feel the heat differently now. He pushed it higher, then lower, then higher again.

"You learn quickly." Morcant said as he watched on.

"It is the only way I know to survive," Airic responded.

He continued in this manner for a long time, changing the height of the flames. He began casting fire over to the stream, launching explosive steam into the air. Morcant soon lost interest and began working his way through his own powerset; forming ice into blades or making various areas of grass turn to frost. The next few hours were spent honing their crafts, and it left Airic feeling a new sense of control.

"What is next?" Airic said, excited to move along in training.

"No, you must never jump from lesson to lesson. Instead, you must learn the first lesson, let it seep into you, and only then can you move on."

Airic chose not to question Morcant. Instead, they headed back to his home, leaving Airic time to focus on the things he had just learned.

24 January, 1113

We trained every day for a week, from the moment the sun rose above the hills until it fell again. There are many chores to do, both before and after training. My hands have become even harder skinned than they were from battle. I keep my distance from Morcant's family, even as they bring me food and fresh clothing. I feel it is only respectful. Morcant has shared more about his battles and involvement with the king, and my mind is nearly set. I have fought it over and over, but I believe the king may be behind my father's death. For now, I will train and grow stronger. Our sessions were cut short today, as a strong wind began to move in, the clouds darkened, and we knew the storm was not far behind. Tonight, we will rest, and return to the fields tomorrow.

The storm had rolled in quickly, catching Morcant, his family, and Airic off guard. Morcant's wife invited Airic in, rather than leaving him to the elements within the barn. He graciously, and hastily, gathered his things, and brought them inside. For a long time, they all sat around a makeshift fireplace and talked about their pasts.   The storm grew into a roar later in the night. Elyana had fallen asleep against her mother's side, and even Alara herself was beginning to doze off. The men were deep into a conversation when a thunderous knock shook the house. Airic and Morcant were each on their feet instantly, braced to fight. They made eye contact and nodded in understanding; Airic quickly moved to the back of the doorway as Morcant prepared to open it. The door creaked open, and the burst of air from the storm pushed through the room, waking Elyana up. Alara grasped her close as she watched the scene unfolding in the doorway.

Two large men, covered in mud and wearing various pieces of armor stood on the steps. Their beards were dripping water, and they each had swords hanging at their sides. Morcant took in the scene as lightning flashed. He could see that more men standing a ways off in the distance.

"Greetings! We are here to ask for your help." One of the men spoke up, his voice gruff and low.
It was hard to place the accent, but Airic and Morcant both knew it was no one they knew.

"What can I do for you?" Morcant asked his hand on the door frame.

"As you can see, it is a bit treacherous. We are seeking shelter for ourselves and some of our men." The man said, gesturing back toward the other group of men, still hidden in the darkness.

"You can use the barn" Morcant offered, offering a light smile. The man at the door ran his eyes through the room and made eye contact with Alara. Morcant noticed the look and tapped lightly on the door, where his other arm sat. He was letting Airic know how many men there were. Morcant moved, cutting off the man's view of his wife. "You can use the barn..." Morcant said again, a bit more stern.

"Aye, the barn" the man responded as he backed down the steps, still looking at Morcant. As he turned to walk to the other men, Morcant closed the door, looking over at Airic.

"What do you think?" Airic asked.

"I think it will be a long night," Morcant responded.

For a long while that night, they could hear nothing but the wind and the occasional shout from the men seemingly having a good time in the barn. Airic and Morcant were both on edge, knowing the longer the men drank, and the longer they stayed awake, the bolder they would become. It was in the early morning hours that another thunderous slamming on the front door began. Alara had taken Elyana to bed much earlier, leaving the two men to sit by the fire and listen. Morcant rushed to the door, with Airic returning to his earlier post on the other side of it. The door creaked open...

"Is there something I can do for you?" Morcant said, looking over the man from earlier in the night. He had obviously spent the night drinking, the stench of the alcohol pouring from his breath.

"The men and I were discussing the chill of the wind. We wondered if we might find some warmth by your fire." The man said, gesturing his arm loosely inside.

"I would be uncomfortable with that, I suggest you return to the barn and be on your way in the morning." Morcant's response was stern, leaving the man processing his denial.

"Maybe I will find warmth in the bed with your wife

then..." The man said with slurred speech.

"Sir, you are drunk, and I once again implore you to return to the barn," Morcant responded coldly as he slowly pushed the door shut. The man braced his foot in the doorway, stopping it from closing all the way.

"I will take what I please" the man barked.

"You will die trying" Morcant hissed back.

The man pushed against the door, moving Morcant backward by the force. Morcant grasped the man's arm as it swung toward his face, dodging left to stop the impact. The man's arm began to turn to ice as Morcant tightened his grip, pushing back and out of the doorway. As he did, the man tumbled backward down the steps. Rolling away from Morcant, he leaped to his feet and grasped his arm.

"Black magic!" He screamed as the other men began to pour out of the barn.

"You won't like how this ends", Morcant shouted as Airic appeared in the doorway behind him.

The man drew his sword and rushed toward Morcant. As he swiped the blade down, it clanged hard against the blunt side of Morcant's arm, encased in a thick layer of ice. Airic had rushed down the stairs, his arms glowing bright against the dark of night.

"They are both witches!" One of the men shouted as the group ran toward them. He slid past Morcant and jumped toward the soldiers. Airic dove in toward one of the men, who was swinging an axe at him. He grasped the handle of the axe and pushed his shoulder into the man's chest. The axe burst into flames, causing the man to screech in terror as he dropped the weapon. Airic spun around and kicked the man back toward the barn. He turned just in time to dodge the blade of a sword, ducking out of the way as it whizzed by his head. He shot fire down onto the ground at the man's feet. It went out quickly in the rain, but it was bright enough to confuse the man. Airic lunged in, grabbing the sword and twisting it back, cutting the man in the stomach. He keeled over into a lump on the ground, and Airic looked back in Morcant's direction.

Morcant punched the side of the large brute in front of him; his arm almost hammer-like with ice. The man was relentless, and elbowed Morcant in the head, causing him to stumble backward. He caught himself on the heel of his foot, then swung his arm up, stopping the attack of the sword once again. He grabbed the collar of the man and squeezed it hard, turning the fabric to ice. He punched up into the man's chin and grabbed his face. The man's eyes lit up in horror as the cold overtook him. The water dripping from his beard, his clothing turned to icicles, forcing him to cry out in pain as he froze. His scream was cut short and turned into a final breath of vapor, slipping out and dissipating in the air.

The group of men stood together in horror, looking at their fallen leaders, eyes widened as they went silent. They turned together and ran off into the woods, screaming of devils and magic, and praying for forgiveness. Morcant and Airic both looked at each other, then down their bodies, and finally back to each other again.

"You fought well," Morcant replied, already moving to grab the body of the assailant at his feet.

"It felt... amazing," Airic responded, walking back toward the other man.

The next half of an hour was spent in total silence, as each body was carried into the distance, out of view of Morcant's home. They took palettes of wood and laid them out, covering them just enough for them to stay dry enough to ignite. Airic took hold of the one closest to him and watched as it burst into flames. Each of them stood for a long time, not speaking, and Morcant bowed his head and said a silent prayer. Finally, he looked up at Airic.

"We will never speak of this." He said coldly.

"Aye," Airic responded.

18 February, 1113

Everything we have been through and accomplished in the weeks past drew a familiar kinship between myself and Morcant. I have learned much about my powers and my abilities to control them. Still, the more I learn about my abilities, the more I desire to get back to the kingdom I had left. There are so many questions that I have yet to answer. My prayers are that Father Williford has been able to get closer to the truth. I struggle to maintain control over my rage, but the more in tune I become with this fire, the more I can push off any actions that will give away my intent.

Airic awoke as the thundering wave of fiery debris crashed over his head. He covered his eyes to keep any dust and smoke from impairing his vision. As he regained focus, he looked up to see the morning sky, a brilliant combination of oranges, purples, and blues. The barn around him was crackling as the blaze grabbed onto the wooden structure. He launched himself up and shuffled in the smoke for his sword. Even through all the chaos and fire, he could hear screams piercing through the air. He rushed toward the doorway of the barn and thrust it open, leaping out as the roof caved in behind him.

A few hundred yards away, Airic could make out the silhouettes of his own army in the morning brightness. He saw a man on his knees and knew instantly, it was Morcant. His house was on fire, and Airic struggled to try and find any signs of Morcant's wife and child. His concentration was broken by the voice of Ayleth, one of the knights.

"Airic, you are alive. Praise the gods!" His hand grasped the neck of Morcant, who was eyeing Airic through the blood that poured down his face. Airic's first instinct was to go on the attack; his hand slipped down his side to find his sword. Morcant moved his head against the soldier's grasp, signaling Airic not to start a fight.

"The king will be pleased to hear of your survival against these monsters."

"There needs to be no bloodshed here. I will return with you and face this man with dignity on the battlefield." Airic kept his voice steady, an attempt at raising no suspicion of his plea.

"There is no room to warrant another day of life for this creature. He will be one less man to fight against us."

Ayleth raised his sword and pierced it through the chest of Morcant. Crying out in agony, Morcant gripped the arms of his executioner and looked into his eyes.

"You will die as you have lived, a coward," Morcant muttered.

He fell back, the sword still in Ayleth's hand. Airic gripped the hilt of his sword, his tongue being fiercely bit in his mouth.

"There is no honor in what you have done here," Airic said.

"Honor? No, this was not about honor. It was about harboring no tolerance for the wicked. It was about another step toward victory in this war."

"What will you tell the king?" Airic questioned.

"He will hear of your life and freedom and will return his gratitude to these men who have rescued you."

The moment was suspended like a point thrust outside of time, yet Airic let his anger pass. He needed Ayleth to trust him, so he could find if it was true that the king had his father killed.

26 February, 1113

Never had I wanted to disappear from a place quite as badly as I do now! I am trying to prepare my mind for the festivities tonight, but I am too focused on the loss of Morcant and the journey back. I had to pretend to harbor no love for my captors, even as Morcant's wife and his child screamed in despair at the murder of their beloved. I have carried those screams with me in battle, and it tortures me when I lay my head to rest. With everything that has happened, a fire has ignited within me. Yes, a new fervor to uncover the plot that has led to such bloodshed of those around me.

The hall bustled with excitement, women in gowns, drunken men in their gluttony, and servants in their despair. Airic was seated to the left side of the king, Ayleth to his right. Another victory on the battlefield meant another feast.

"Come on gents. We are one step closer to kingdom come!" The king's voice thundered as he smiled and shouted, droplets of wine falling away from his beard.

"It was a long fight, but aye, our army has never looked stronger," Ayleth replied.

"What say you, Airic?" The king's voice dropped to a much more commanding tone.

Airic had grown tired of the seemingly endless war, and everything he thought he had been fighting for. None of it mattered to him anymore, only getting to the bottom of his father's murder. His trust had waned in nearly every person, even as the king continued to lift him up. He was angry; for the murder of his father, for the execution of Morcant, and for knowing that the people responsible were here in this room.

"Their army was outwitted, weak, and disorganized. It was a swift, simple battle that cost us barely any resources" Airic replied. The king, and Ayleth, both looked at him with furrowed brows. At last, the king spoke.

"Aye, but we looked good, did we not?" The king's question made Airic realize his tone. He gathered his thoughts before answering, deliberating a way out of the conversation.

"It is true. I must apologize. I feel a touch of the sweating sickness," Airic said as he raised himself from the table.

"Go find a woman to calm your nerves, Airic," the king responded as he raised a broken turkey leg to his mouth. Airic bowed and made his way to the back of the hall and through the doors. The guards nodded as he left, and he returned the notion.

As Airic headed toward his room, he passed by the open doorway to the study of Father Williford. He leaned into the doorway and looked around. He spotted the reverend huddled at a small table in the corner, in front of some books.

"Father Williford, why are you not attending the party?" he asked, not because he was unaware of the answer, but because he wanted his presence to be known.

"Ah, Airic, you know I do not waste my mind with such things," he responded. He turned to face Airic with a book in one hand and a leather flask in the other.

"What is occupying your time this evening?" The question was followed by a moment of silence as Williford rustled past Airic to close the large wooden door to the hallway. He turned as it shut and placed the flask on the small desk that rested underneath the torch. It slumped over to fall on the edge of a small plate, with untouched food that was obviously from the Great Hall.

"I have been working on our little investigation, scouring through notes and old records. I believe you may be onto something with what your friend told you," He said. His eyes wandered around the room as he moved back over to the table.

"So, it was the king then?"

"I am not so sure. I can see no benefit to such an act for him. However, I also do not claim to have the full picture."

"What do we know?"

"Only a select few knew of the Horn of Valkyr's existence. That is the name used over and over for the group your father had led. They were sent into specific battles, to have a direct impact with the use of their magic."

"You do believe this is a spell of some sort?" Airic asked, holding his hands up between the two men.

"Even God's Word speaks of magic, but it does not mean I

condone of such things. I know of no other explanation."

"Where do we go from here? How can I avenge my family if we do not even know who was behind this?" Airic said, a light glow emanating from his face and hands. Williford put his hand out as if an attempt to settle the rage with his own hand.

"You should never rush into anything, Airic. Instead, watch and wait. The light reveals everything that is shrouded in darkness but only in its own time. "Williford's response angered Airic; and, had he not been a holy man, it could have sent him into a rage. He knew that Williford was only trying to help him, but he was tired of waiting, boiling in anger.

Father Williford was busy, his nose buried deep into another book. Airic stood by, watching him for a moment, finally turning to walk away.

"Watch, and wait..." Williford said.

"Thank you for being there for me, Father. I would know even less than I do now, had it not been for you." Airic responded, pausing at the doorway before moving out and into the hallway.

I have found myself growing more tired of the battle. It sparks no love inside of me. Too many dark things are going on behind the veil. The darkness is consuming my every thought. My trust of everyone around me has waned thin, and I do not care to spend time with any of them. Still, until I can know for sure, I will serve the King, if not for him, for the kingdom of people who have done me no wrong.

Airic pushed himself up from the ground, the cold wind cutting through his thick coat. All around him were the screams of battle and death. He parried to his right and pushed the hilt of his sword against the back of a large-hulking brute. The man turned and slammed a large mace into Airic's shield, sending him skidding backward with the intensity of the hit. He ducked out of the way as the weapon swung over his head. Airic drove his blade against the leg of the man. Without a scream, and seemingly unphased, the man turned and lumbered toward Airic. As he raised his arm to crush Airic with the weapon, Airic pushed his blade up into the man's wrist; and moved out of the way as the mace, still being held by the now detached hand, fell to the ground beside them both. The man screamed out in pain, and reached with his other hand and grabbed Airic's collar and pulled him from the ground. He began to furiously beat his head against Airic's helmet, leaving Airic confused for a moment. He finally planted his feet against the man's torso and pushed away with all his might, flailing backward as he swiped his sword out with one hand. He crashed to the ground, quickly scrambling to regain his footing. He turned and looked at the man, who now stood motionless, a deep gash along his throat. His body finally collapsed and fell to the ground, a spray of blood covering the snow below.

Around him, Airic watched as the men clashed, crashing into each other and fighting until the other was lifeless. The snow fell in a blistering fury, coating the ground and the bodies which laid there. The two armies had never met in battle before this moment, and each side was stacking up its pile of dead. It had been two days of an intense battle, and neither army had backed down. Airic thought that it was admirable, but he was exhausted all the same. He pushed on in the battle, with his sword covered in the blood of his enemies. His mind kept flipping back to the battle he had with Morcant, and the moment he had realized he was not alone with his powers. Now, he suppressed them to be sure no one would know anything of his ability. He remembered the moments outside of Morcant's home when they stood side by side and fought off the horde of gruesome men who attacked them. He had never felt so at ease than letting the fire take over, and he missed it so. On occasion, he would rush off into the woods and maintain his practice, leaving various parts of nearby fields scorched. The men whispered of dragons, which amused him; but, he said nothing.

The battle lasted late into the night, forcing each of the men to push deeper into the throngs of battle, lit only by the moon and various fires. Airic was growing disgusted in himself, longing to use his powers, but forced to keep the secret intact. He was angry at himself, Ayleth, and the King. It was nearly too much to keep in, and he caught himself beginning to glow faintly. Those around him were too caught up in the bloodshed to notice, but he knew he had to find control. He began to move his way to the end of the battlefield, fighting through the crowd and striking down the enemies that moved against him. He could feel the pumping adrenaline inside of him, and he struggled to focus. It was as if the screams were growing louder, desperate to break through the clangs of metal and bustling fires.

He finally broke through the last lines of the battlefield. He made his way to the line of trees, out of sight of anyone around him. He held his chest as he tried to catch his breath, as the cold air felt like daggers of ice pushing into his lungs. He steadied himself against a large tree and closed his eyes, a desperate attempt to center himself. After a moment, the ringing in his ears stopped, and his skin stopped glowing.

As he rested, he noticed a few voices traveling through the

air. He followed them, pushing past the brush and twigs to find its source. Every step he took closer allowed him to hear a bit more of the conversation. Within a few moments, he realized one of the voices was that of Ayleth. He kneeled behind a large stone and peered over it to see what was happening. Ayleth was standing with a group of ten soldiers, each in pristine and unrustled armor and weaponry. It was obvious to Airic that these men had not seen the battle. A small fire was beside them, with a makeshift battle tent, a table, and various items atop it.

"Sir, it appears the battle is nearly over, and our men were too much for their forces," said a gruff, large soldier.

"This is excellent news. How many have we lost?" Ayleth questioned, an eyebrow raised.

"Six thousand, sir." The man responded shakily. It grew quiet for a moment, and Airic thought they were taking a moment of silence.

"Acceptable! Return to your posts," Ayleth quickly shot out. The men each turned and began to make their way out of sight. One of the men, a small, lightly armored soldier, stayed behind.

"Anything to report?" Ayleth asked.

"I saw nothing, but I also lost sight of him." The soldier responded as Ayleth looked off and to the ground.

"We need to keep tabs on him. If he displays anything his father did, the king must be alerted immediately...through me." Ayleth barked his command at the man, who turned and walked away. Airic turned his back to the rock, stunned at the realization that he had just heard. The king was behind his father's murder; he now had no doubt. He clenched his fists and walked back through the woods to the battlefield, deciding it was time to end this battle himself.

21 November, 1113

There is a rage inside of me, one that was born in fire and flame. I believe it is the same that burned within my father, and that I have quenched for far too long. I do not know what the day holds, but Ayleth has confirmed my deepest fear, that King Henry is behind the death of my father. I have served under this man for years, killing for a kingdom that turned its back on my family. The depths of poison from this place is more than I can bear. I have stayed my hand for far too long, allowing these acts to go unpunished. Today, the King will pay, the kingdom will pay, and I will have my revenge.

The doors of the throne room erupted into splinters of fire and ash, sparking as they hit the stone floors. The king was forced back into the seat of his throne as the guards rushed to guard him. Ayleth moved to the front of their blades, pointing toward Airic as he screamed to the king.

"The traitor has come to kill you, my king!" His voice echoed through the chamber, an attempt at silencing Airic.

"You... you had my father killed! He was a knight in your army!" Airic's skin was glowing bright, fire flowing across his fingertips. The guards shifted their feet in fear as he inched closer. The king stood and ran his hands over his tunic, straightening the fabric.

"Your father was a loyal knight, a man I considered a friend. Yet you, his son, who I took in and raised in his honor, dares to come to threaten the very king he served?"

"A friend wouldn't have those he loved murdered; only a coward would do that."

"You will bite your tongue or you will lose it! You accuse me as a coward but know nothing of what you speak. Your father was killed in battle, as a warrior." His voice thundered with authority, the floor seeming to shake with his power.

"He was killed by your men, not some foreign enemy. Killed because you found out about his powers." Airic stepped forward again, his grip tightening around the handle of his sword.

"I knew about his powers. He led my army because of those powers. Now, you will stop where you stand, or I will have you struck down." Ayleth moved forward, drawing his sword as the king spoke.

Airic's mind swam in confusion, drowning in the conversations he had with Morcant, with the things he had uncovered. He narrowed his gaze toward the king allowing the fire subside across his skin.

"When my father fell, who came to lead your men?" The king did not speak, but instead, he gestured toward Ayleth. In Airic's mind, the pieces began to fall into place.

"You, all along it was you. The only person that stood to gain from my father's death. How could I have been so blind?" As Airic spoke, Ayleth rushed toward him. His blade sliced into the air as Airic slipped out of the way.

"That is enough!" His voice cracked into the air. Airic drew his sword, lifting it in time to block the next blow from the raging Ayleth.

"The king's greatest warrior, and leader. You knew you could never move up if my father stood in the way. You sent those men in to kill him!" Airic lunged at Ayleth, pushing his shoulder into his chest, launching him backward into the guards. The sword flew from Ayleth's hands, then landed with a clank against the floor. He jumped to his feet and slid behind the guards, pushing one of them forward.

"He has to be stopped!" He yells. The king raises his hand as the guards look back at him for approval. They lower their swords.

"Ayleth, is this true?" The king's voice is no longer thundering, instead, it is soft and low, dripping with inquisitive anger.

"My king, he-he is a liar! Arden was my friend, my general." Ayleth stepped before the throne.

"Morcant, you killed him because he knew. He recognized you. Instead of taking him prisoner, you murdered him." Airic stared at the ground, reflecting on everything he had faced, all the things he had learned. It all became so clear at this moment.

"He was the enemy! He had taken you hostage and I freed

you!" Ayleth's voice begins to crack.

"He told you he remembered your face. Right before you killed him. He had told me that someone had come to him with an offer of peace if he killed my father, but he refused. It was you!"

The king stood, watching as the men shared their words, struggling through it in his own mind. He looked to Airic, then back at Ayleth.

"You told me Morcant attacked you, and you killed him."

"He...I...Enough." Alyeth lunged at the king, spinning around behind him as a dagger appeared from his sleeve. He placed the blade against the king's neck, pulling him back against his chest. The guards spun around in confusion, raising their swords towards him. Airic stepped forward, now behind the soldiers.
"You betray your king?" The room fell silent as if the air in it had been sucked out. Everyone stood on edge, knowing that these moments would change everything. Airic quenched his rage, pushing it away as he began to think of a way to save the king. He watched as Ayleth's eyes shifted back and forth, an acknowledgement that he had gone too far, and had no idea what he would do next. The king's teeth were clenched tightly not because of a fear for the blade at his throat, but because of his own anger.

"You, and your kind, are mistakes! Vessels of darkness; trying to rule humanity in fear!" Ayleth's anger forced tears to well up in his eyes.

Airic's fists were clenched, building his rage and strength. The second he released it, he knew he had to move quickly. In a moment, the room filled with light, and flame, as Airic finally let go. The white heat of fire erupted from his core, the candles in the throne room igniting in a bright flash. All at once, the guards, Ayleth, and the king each shielded their eyes from the light. Airic moved in, pushing past the guards as the fire died. He pulled Ayleth's arm down while pushing his body into the king to move him away from the blade. Ayleth flailed out in anger and defense; dropping the blade to the ground, he lunged for it, rolling onto the floor. Airic swings his sword from its sheath, grazing against the face of his enemy. Ayleth launched himself up, grabbing the dagger and twisting it toward Airic. He touched the back of his hand to his face, wiping away the fresh blood. He lunged forward, driving his knee into Airic's stomach and slammed his hand against the hilt of the sword. The two men fell together, rolling down the steps in front of the throne. Both men clamored to regain their footing, Airic reached out and grasped Ayleth's throat. Fire ran down Airic's arms to his fingertips, and the smell of burning flesh was creating a dysphoric air in the room.

"Aggghhhh!" Ayleth screamed as his neck began to burn. He pulled his arm back and plunged the dagger into Airic's stomach.

"Ughn" is all Airic could muster as the men both fell to their knees.

"You... die... here... with me..." Ayleth gasped between each breath. His hair began to fall away, strand by strand, turning to sparks as they each hit the ground. The blood from Airic's side sizzled as it fell to the concrete floor.

"I will escort you to Hell's gates then." Airic's body began to shine brighter, turning the whole corridor white. His clothing burned away, and his armor shifted its shape against the heat. Ayleth screamed one last time as he turned to ash and fell through Airic's hands. He turned to the king, gripped his wound, and fell.

"Get him to the physician, now!" The king screamed. The guards were finally able to react as they snapped back to reality. They each took off, leaving the king kneeling beside Airic.

24 November, 1113

I do not know who might someday find this journal. Perhaps there will have been a story or two attached to its ownership. Let it be known that I am not proud of the things I have done, but I carry the weight of those decisions with me. I believed the king to be a vile rat, only to realize he was the friend of my father. Ayleth, my father's right-hand man, had betrayed him and had him killed. He feared the powers he possessed and thought he could establish his own reign by stamping out what he was scared of. If you allow the fear of who someone else is capable of becoming to run your life, you will only use your humanity.

Airic secured the leather journal with its strap and dropped the quill to the floor. Everything fell silent as the darkness of night took hold. He paused for a moment, lying there in his bed. The candle flickered, causing shadows to dance around the walls of the room. He watched for a moment, his head still swimming from the physician's potions. He clutched his wound and coughed, forcing his body to turn toward the window at the same time. He could see the moon clearly, shining brightly in the sky. He smiled, wondering again if his mother and sister were looking at the beautiful view at the same time. He slipped the journal onto the wooden table beside him, closed his eyes, and found his rest.

The woods were dark, but the moonlight was enough to shine through the tops of the trees onto the dirt below. Sounds of trampling feet, scurrying their way through the forest, filled the air. Grunts from angry men, slashing their way through the brush and thistles as they marched toward their target.

A young husband and wife pushed their way deeper into the woods, desperate to escape the angry mob behind them. The man frantically tried to shield the torch from the wind caused by their sprinting. It was no use, and in a moment, the light was gone. The couple continued to run as he released the torch to the ground behind them. Their hands clasped together as they shuffled over branches and leaves, pulling each other further away from the mob.

It almost seemed that they would get away, until the man tripped, sending him spiraling over and dragging the woman down behind him. He grasped his leg, knowing immediately it was broke. They pulled close to each other and tried to remain as silent as possible. Still, the mob inched ever closer, their torches lighting up more of the forest floor.

"What do we do now?" The man asked, looking into the eyes of his wife.

"I... I am done running." She said, standing up slowly and turning to face the mob.

"There they are!" One of the men yelled, turning the entire crowd in the direction of the couple. The voices grew louder, their anger blasting through the air. As they closed in on the couple, the woman put her hands out.

"Please, leave us alone. We will never come back, just let us go." She cried out to them.

"We can not let you get away, witches must be dealt with, lest you try and destroy our village!" Another man screamed out.

"I am no witch!" She exclaimed, her own anger growing.

"Take her down..." A gruff voice said from somewhere beside her.

She turned quickly and balled up her fist, pulling her arm back and thrusting hard, punching hard into the trunk of a large tree. The bark turned to ice around her fist, and within an instant the whole tree was encased in ice. The wood crackled under the sudden change in pressure, before bursting into a falling cloud of ice and snow. Below, the crowd held their arms up to shield themselves from the falling debris. Torches went out instantly, and the people were covered in a thick layer of snow.

"WITCH!" A woman yelled as she hurtled a rock, crushing it into the arm of the young woman. She grasped her arm as she fell backward. Her husband stood behind her, bracing her as he held onto her.

"We have to kill her!" Someone else yelled. The man and woman looked at each other as she leaned against him. He searched her eyes, trying to find any glimmer of hope or another way out.

"Do it." He said calmly.

She turned to face the crowd once again, more rocks hurled in her direction. She touched the ground, and it turned to ice. In seconds the ice crawled over the legs of the people in the crowd. Their cries of anger quickly turned to desperate screams as the ice climbed over their torso's and necks. The woman looked away, waiting for the silence to take over again. Soon, there were only the sounds of crackling ice, settling against the ground.

"Sarai, we have to go. Now!" The man said as he grabbed her arm and pulled her up. She put her arm under his and propped him up as they shuffled on into the night.

She raised her eyes up to the moon, watching it come in and out of view as they moved through the woods.

"I am so sorry" she whispered.

THE END